Y0-DWO-739

FRANCESCA DAFNE VIGNAGA

IGOR

WINDMILL
BOOKS ™

Published in 2021 by Windmill Books, an Imprint of Rosen Publishing
29 East 21st Street, New York, NY 10010

Copyright © 2021 for this book in English language published by Rosen Publishing
Original Italian edition © 2018 Edizioni Corsare

Text and Illustrations by Francesca Dafne Vignaga
Published by arrangement with Atlantyca S.p.A.

Cataloging-in-Publication Data

Names: Vignaga, Francesca Dafne.
Title: Igor / Francesca Dafne Vignaga.
Description: New York : Windmill Books, 2021. |
Identifiers: ISBN 9781499486582 (pbk.) | ISBN 9781499486599 (library bound) | ISBN
9781499486858 (6 pack) | ISBN 9781499486605 (ebook)
Subjects: LCSH: Friendship–Juvenile fiction. | Monsters–Juvenile fiction.
Classification: LCC PZ7.1.V546 Ig 2021 | DDC [E]–dc23

Manufactured in the United States of America

CPSIA Compliance Information: Batch #BS20WM. For Further Information contact Rosen Publishing, New York, New York at 1-800-237-9932.

Find us on

Name: Igor

Born: October 24

Address: The first branch to the right of the third ginkgo biloba tree from the left.

Height:
Four inches (depending on how messy his fur is)

Distinguishing features:

Very furry and smiles a lot

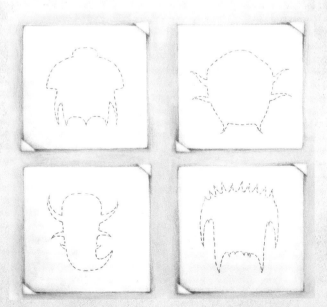

Paw print

4

This is Igor.

The only thing he knows about himself is his name.

He can do magic tricks with flowers and seeds.

He can make a whistle out of a leaf.

And he can climb trees – even very tall ones.

8

When he is not busy playing, he likes to watch what the animals do:
long lines of ants carrying heavy loads,
cats hiding in the grass,
sparrows splashing in puddles.

9

But Igor has been wondering about something for a few days:

Why has he never seen anyone like him?

Maybe there is someone somewhere. He just needs to go look for them.

Maybe it is time to leave home and go on a journey.

11

15

18

19

21

23

28

Igor is happy to have met another creature like him, but he cannot stay.

He has so many things to do and see.

Igor will never forget his new friend.

He will come back to see him and send a postcard from every place he visits.

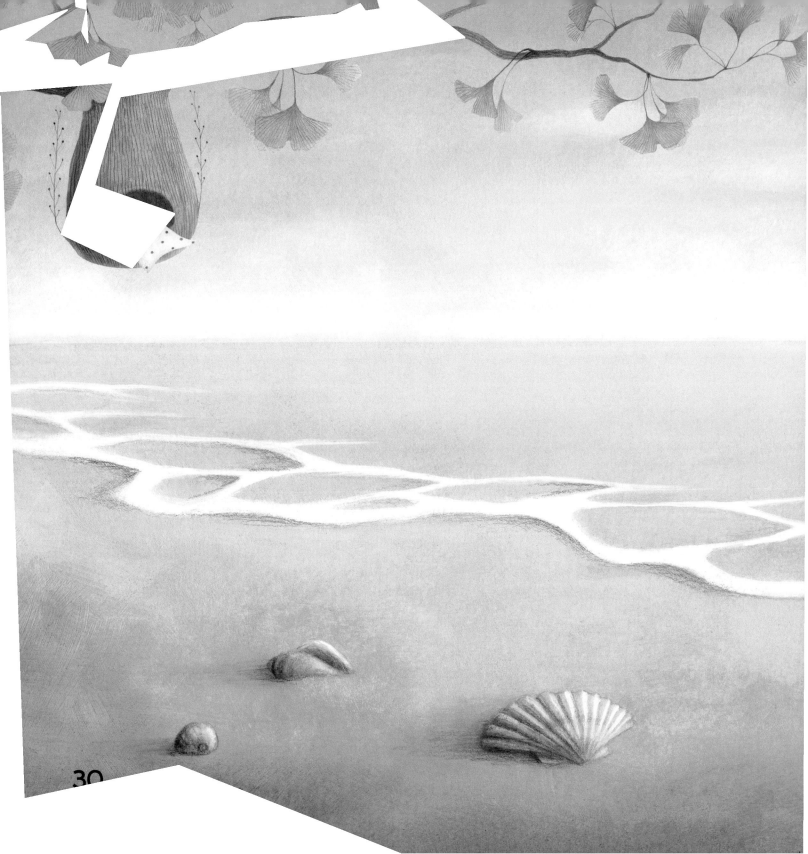

Now Igor is a little tired. So, he decides to go home to rest and listen to his favorite music.

He is happy and already dreaming about his next journey.

Name: Igor

Born: October 24

Address: The first branch to the right of the third ginkgo biloba tree from the left.

Height:
Four inches (depending on how messy his fur is)

Distinguishing features:

Very furry and smiles a lot

Paw print